Children's Books:
A Mermaid Tea Party

Sally Huss

ISBN: 0692355464
ISBN 13: 9780692355466

Maggie the Mermaid was awakened one morning by her mother.

"Get up! Get up! It's time for school!"

"Yes, yes," smiled Maggie, as she sat up. She remembered that this was the day her teacher was going to teach the class about having a tea party.

Quickly she straightened herself, smoothed her scales, combed her hair, and swam to the breakfast table.

Her mother had prepared her favorite breakfast...

... seaweed cereal topped with berry wrack, sugar kelp, whale milk, and scrambled fish eggs on a piece of toast made from nori.

After gobbling it all down and thanking her mother, she put on her backpack... and headed out the grotto doorway.

She passed a cave where a moray eel hid. She kept her distance.

She waved to a passing school of fish that were on their way to their own school. "Good morning, Maggie!" each said as they passed by.

A friendly dolphin stopped to ask if she wanted a ride. He could see that she was in a hurry.

"Yes, thank you," she said; then grabbed his fin, and they were off.

When they reached the tall reeds to the entrance of the school, Maggie thanked the dolphin, slid from his back, and greeted her friends.

The mermaids were all atwitter. They were going to have a tea party! They had all had birthday parties and been to 4th of July parties and other holiday parties, but not to a tea party. This was going to be really special.

After taking roll call and saying the Pledge of Allegiance to the flag (they all pledged to keep their ocean clean), Miss Crandall led them over to a big, round table.

There it was — a party table fit for a queen! Beautifully colored sea anemones made up the centerpiece. Lacey seaweed served as the tablecloth and there were even matching napkins! Delicate tuna sandwiches lay gracefully on platters of mother-of-pearl. Puffy sweet clam cakes sat on elegant mollusk trays. Dainty slices of seal cheese decorated brown algae sea crackers. Little oyster shell china bowls held after-tea mints made from kelp.

Then there was the tea set: cups and saucers, a sugar bowl and creamer, and the grand focus of the day – the teapot! Yes, the star of the party was the teapot – not just what it held, but what it meant!

The mermaids seated themselves around the table. Each had an obliging turtle for a stool.

    Miss Crandall began, "First take your napkins and put them on your laps." They all did as they were told. "No elbows on the table, please," she added.

Then, as Miss Crandall held up one cup to be filled, she

explained, "A tea party is not just about tea and crumpets, it is

about kindness and appreciation. As I fill this cup with tea, I am

filling it with my good wishes for the one who receives it. As I take

care of how I handle the teacup and the teapot (and the mermaids could see that she was), I fill the cup with care for the one who receives it. In this way it becomes a gift."

Next, Miss Crandall passed the teacup with its saucer to the mermaid to her left. That mermaid held it carefully as well, and when she passed it on, her kindness was added to the cup of tea.

Each mermaid took the cup respectfully, and in turn passed it to the next, always adding her appreciation to it.

Maggie was last in the line and received the cup gratefully. She had sat patiently waiting as all the other mermaids were served their cups of tea.

While the pouring and passing was going on, Miss Crandall continued, explaining, "It is important that when you offer a container to another it must have something in it. It must never be empty.

Whether it's a cup, a bowl, or a sand bucket. It must have something in it. We never want to offer emptiness to another. In this case, we are offering tea, but tea with a special ingredient – our loving kindness."

All the mermaids looked at each other, realizing that they were learning something more than how to pour tea. They paid close attention.

Next as the party continued, Miss Crandall had the mermaids pass plates and the trays of food around. As each tray was passed, more kindness was shared.

Politely, and ever so carefully, each mermaid took from the trays just what she needed and no more, leaving plenty for the others.

As the mermaids nibbled and sipped, they agreed tea and sandwiches had never tasted so good.

Then as the party came to a close, it was time to clean up.

The party was over, but was it? As the mermaids cleared the table and washed the dishes, they took the same care with the cups and saucers, plates and platters as they had when they were filled with food. Not a dish was chipped, not a harsh word was spoken. Only a few giggles and singing were heard.

As the mermaids left school that day, each continued to practice her good manners by thanking their teacher for the party.

And Miss Crandall in turn replied, "You are most welcome." Giving and receiving kind words was a part of their day's lesson.

That afternoon when Maggie returned home, she took the lessons she had learned that day at the tea party with her. She helped her mother straighten the grotto and prepare for dinner, all the while caring about what she was doing.

With everything she touched she added her loving kindness to it, whether it was dusting the furniture or setting the table. She did it happily, making her own party out of it.

Yes, the mermaid tea party that day with Miss Crandall was just the beginning of endless parties every mermaid could have by being kind, careful, and appreciative. And Maggie, like all the mermaids, now knew how to do it!

The End, but not
the end of being
kind and appreciative

    At the end of this book you will find a Certificate of Merit that may be issued to any girl who promises to honor the requirements stated in the Certificate. This fine Certificate will easily fit into a 5"x7" frame, and happily suit any girl who receives it!

Here is another adorable book by Sally Huss.

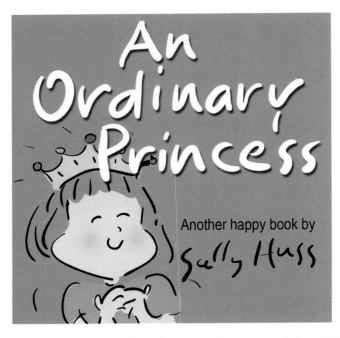

Synopsis: Laura Sue wanted to be a princess with all her heart. However, she was not from a royal family; she was from an ordinary family, which included an ordinary brother.

One day to her delight, her teacher announced to the students that they could be anything they wanted to be. This was music to Laura Sue's ears, until she announced her desire in front of the class. Laughter dampened her spirits, as did the reality that her family members offered. However, a beautiful, golden angel came to her rescue and told her how to become an ordinary princess. The angel gave her the formula and it is one every child could follow should he or she wish to become an ordinary prince or princess.

From AN ORDINARY PRINCESS -- http://amzn.com/B00N1IR0IS.

If you liked A MERMAID TEA PARTY, please be kind enough to post a short review on Amazon by using this URL: http://amzn.com/B0086IAPGW.

You may wish to join our Family of Friends to receive information about upcoming FREE e-book promotions and download a free poster – The Importance Happiness on Sally's website -- http://www.sallyhuss.com. Thank You.

More Sally Huss books may be viewed on the Author's Profile on Amazon. Here is that URL: http://amzn.to/VpR7B8.

About the Author/Illustrator

Sally Huss

"Bright and happy," "light and whimsical" have been the catch phrases attached to the writings and art of Sally Huss for over 30 years. Sweet images dance across all of Sally's creations, whether in the form of children's books, paintings, wallpaper, ceramics, baby bibs, purses, clothing, or her King Features syndicated newspaper panel "Happy Musings."

Sally creates children's books to uplift the lives of children and hopes you will join her in this effort by helping spread her happy messages.

Sally is a graduate of USC with a degree in Fine Art and through the years has had 26 of her own licensed art galleries throughout the world.

This certificate may be cut out, framed, and presented
to any little girl who promises to honor the princess within her.

Certificate of Merit

(Name)

The girl named above is awarded this Certificate of Merit
for practicing loving kindness whenever possible and
for promising to be:

*Helpful at home and in school
*Grateful at all times
*Friendly to everyone

Presented by: _____

Date: _____

Printed in Great Britain
by Amazon.co.uk, Ltd.,
Marston Gate.